Tiffany

Thanks for the support
Keep reading

Daydream

Tiffany Felix

Copyright © 2019 Tiffany Felix.

All rights reserved. No part of this book may be used or reproduced by any means, graphic, electronic, or mechanical, including photocopying, recording, taping or by any information storage retrieval system without the written permission of the author except in the case of brief quotations embodied in critical articles and reviews.

LifeRich Publishing is a registered trademark of The Reader's Digest Association, Inc.

LifeRich Publishing books may be ordered through booksellers or by contacting:

LifeRich Publishing
1663 Liberty Drive
Bloomington, IN 47403
www.liferichpublishing.com
1 (888) 238-8637

Because of the dynamic nature of the Internet, any web addresses or links contained in this book may have changed since publication and may no longer be valid. The views expressed in this work are solely those of the author and do not necessarily reflect the views of the publisher, and the publisher hereby disclaims any responsibility for them.

This is a work of fiction. All of the characters, names, incidents, organizations, and dialogue in this novel are either the products of the author's imagination or are used fictitiously.

Any people depicted in stock imagery provided by Getty Images are models, and such images are being used for illustrative purposes only.
Certain stock imagery © Getty Images.

ISBN: 978-1-4897-2077-1 (sc)
ISBN: 978-1-4897-2078-8 (e)

Library of Congress Control Number: 2018966926

Print information available on the last page.

LifeRich Publishing rev. date: 01/30/2019

Dedicated to my Mom & Dad. Thank you for all you do.
Special thanks:
To God for loving me
To my extended family for their support
To my church family for being there for me.

In loving memory of my Grand Pa. I miss you.
1934-2018

Prologue

The lights and desks started to shake. The floors were rumbling through the second floor. People started to find shelter underneath the desks to stay away from the falling books. The rattling left the windows shattered across the classroom. But this was no earthquake. Through the confusion, a huge robot with four legs, and clawed hands rises into view in the window panes.

"HHHEEEEELLLLLPPPPP!" somebody from the classroom shrieked in distress.

Jake knew exactly what he is supposed to do. He got out from under the desk and jumped out the broken window. Just when he is about to hit the sidewalk concrete, he flew upward. His striped red and blue shirt became a cape and his denim blue jeans turned into tights. Jake was not Jake anymore, he was CAPABLE. The only superhero who is capable of anything.

The class, watching in, became a sea of surprised faces.

Jake came face to face with the machine as the class began to chant his name.

"Jake! Jake! Jake!..."

But just when Jake was about to throw the first punch...

"Jake Kale, isn't that right?" said the math teacher Mrs. Smith.

"Huh, yeah?" Jake replied.

Everyone else in the class start laughing. Jake turned to his best friend Amanda.

"What exactly did I say yes to?"

"That you will meet her in detention after class."

"Again!"

"This is starting to become a habit of yours."

"It's not my fault. My brain just refuses to listen to the math teacher …. and every other teacher."

"Mr. Kale, do you want to make it two days?" said Ms. Smith now giving Jake the evil eye.

"No ma'am."

Just then the bell rung announcing the end of the day. But to Jake it felt as if the bell was mocking his misery. Mrs. Smith dismissed the class as everybody rushed out the door, except Jake. Jake walked out the door sluggishly, stalling for more time.

Jake has been to detention so many times that he knew the way there by heart.

Jake took his time as he thought to himself:

One-day people will admire that I daydream so much. They would all gather around to hear them.

His thoughts were more accurate than he imagined.

Chapter 1

Jake stared at the room number. He has seen it almost a thousand times.. Room #217. Detention. Where children's nightmares were held. (Okay maybe that was a little dramatic, but you definitely didn't want to be there on a Friday afternoon. That was just pure torture.)

But Jake knew that skipping a detention would resort to a full week of escorted detention and he just didn't need that. Especially being a middle schooler, teachers walking him was not the best for his reputation.

Jake finally caught up with his brain and let himself in.

"Jake, didn't think I'll see you here again." said Ms. Reaper, the detention monitor.

Although she had a sarcastic flare, Ms. Reaper always smiled and was nice to everyone. With Ms. Reaper's blonde hair, Ms. Reaper was the only thing Jake looked forward to when he had detention. The only flaw she had was that she was the English teacher. For Jake that was a big no, no.

Jake smiled at her and handed in his detention slip. Jake turned around to look at who else was there. To his surprise, he was the only one there. Usually there was Norman, who was abnormally normal.

Nobody ever messed with him because they were scared Norman could take them out with a single punch but really, it turned out that Norman was a softie that came late to school sometimes.

But today ,there was nothing but empty chairs.

Jake sat in the seat in the back, the one closest to the door. Once detention was over, he wanted to get out of school as fast as possible.

When Norman and Jake had detention together they usually passed notes and hoped Ms. Reaper didn't give them another detention. But since Norman wasn't here he decided to do his homework.

This may come across as weird but just to make sure you read it right, I'll tell you again. Jake wanted to do his homework. That is usually a last resort for Jake but since Norman wasn't there he was bored. And you didn't want Jake bored.

Jake read his assignment:

Directions :

Write a short story about any topic. It must include at least one setting and characters that may be real or fake. It must have the necessary components of a story. No profanity or inappropriate scenes.

Jake usually thinks his homework is difficult but this was surprisingly easy. Jake just decided to write a story about one of his day dreams.

An hour later, Ms. Reaper tapped Jake on the shoulder.

"Jake, detention is over. You can go now." she said.

Jake must have been so into his story that he didn't even realize that detention ended already. Jake quickly put his things away and walked out of the classroom as fast as he could.

But what Jake didn't see was that Ms. Reaper was looking back at him.

Chapter 2

―൜൜ඐ൜ඐ൜ඐ൜൜―

"Jake, come up please." said Ms. Reaper In English class that day. And sadly Tuesday morning wasn't doing Jake any good. But Jake complied anyway.

"Yes, Ms. Reaper."

"Oh yes, Jake. I read your story and I would really appreciate if you read it to the class."

Now Jake would never say "no" to a teacher. But he was really contemplating it now. After much debate, he made a final decision.

"Sure…" Jake said, not liking what he came up with.

"Attention class, Jake would like to read his story for you." she smiled but to Jake it was deceiving.

Jake was shy at first, but once he started to read the story, all fears went away.

"It was a normal day at the school. It was the last period of the day and all the students were anticipating the last bell but math was holding the kids back from their freedom.

"The students were well into the class when...

BOOM, CRASH

The windows crashed and laid in a pile of rubble on the classroom floor. Through the destruction, the class saw a 20-foot-tall robot staring right back at them.

'HHHEEEEELLLLLPPPPP' screamed somebody from the class.

"Suddenly, one of the kids from the classroom started acting fast. It was Jake! Jake jumped out of the window. But just a second before he splattered onto the hard-concrete sidewalk, he flew upwards.

"His striped blue and red shirt and blue denim jeans turned into tights and a cape. No, Jake wasn't Jake anymore, he was CAPABLE, the only superhero who was capable of anything.

"The whole class stared astonished with their mouths wide open as CAPABLE threw the first punch. The hit made a huge dent in the metal but the robot wasn't going down without a fight.

"It threw its giant clawed hands at the boy. CAPABLE dodged right on time but the momentum made the robot fall over. CAPABLE took the advantage and picked up the robot. He threw it in the air and when it came back down Jake kicked it into space.

"The class cheered as he came back through the window back in his usual attire. But with a snap of his fingers nobody remembered a thing.

"The End"

Chapter 3

Jake couldn't say he was surprised. He definitely wasn't expecting a standing ovation. The laughing and the mocking may have been uncalled for but what did he think was going to happen. He was in seventh grade and was imaging himself as a superhero. He looked back at Ms. Reaper but she avoided his eyes as she proceeded to calm the class down. Jake blushed and slipped back into his seat.

Before he knew it, class was over. It was only the morning and he knew people would be talking about this for the rest of the day. Jake was ready to just slip under the radar to avoid everybody but Ms. Reaper had other ideas.

"Jake, can you come to my desk please?"

Usually when Jake heard these words it ended up with a detention and a phone call home. But that wasn't the case.

"Do you know what you got on your paper?" said Ms. Reaper.

"No."

"Jake, you got an A+."

Jake couldn't hide the surprise. He never got a B before, let alone an A+. Jake tried to say something but nothing came out of his mouth. Finally, he got the courage to muster something.

"Really?" Jake said immediately regretting it.

"This was a great story, I saw you working hard on it in detention and I was surprised. There is a writing competition, and I think you should join."

"A writing competition?"

"Yes, and the winner's story is going to be included in the newspaper. I think it is a good experience and many students in the grade are going to be in the competition too."

Jake didn't know what to say. Did he really want to be on the newspaper?

"You don't have to tell me right away, you can tell me your decision tomorrow."

"Alright, I'll let you know as soon as possible."

And with that they exchanged good-byes and Jake went home with something he really needed to think about.

Chapter 4

―⁓⁓⁓⁓―

"Hey, I'm home." Jake yelled as soon as he got inside the house. Jake and his older brother Drake always walked home together but it seemed like today Jake was a few steps ahead of him.

"Hello ,Jake, how was your day?" Jake's mother responded. She probably got off work early. Usually Jake and Drake's mother got home a few minutes after they arrived home.

"It was good."

Just then, Drake shoved through the door. He greeted their mom, got a snack from the pantry, and immediately went to his room.

"Teenagers." Jake's mother humored.

"We never know what to do with them."

His mother laughed and continued their conversation.

"Did anything exciting happen today?"

It was like Jake's mother could read his mind.

"Actually, my teacher liked my story in class today. I actually got an A+ and she wanted me to join a writing competition."

"Really! Oh honey, that's amazing. Are you going to join? It would be an amazing opportunity."

"Uh, I don't know. I don't normally go for this sort of thing."

"Are you sure? It would be fun. It's something new, and if the story you made for class really was that good, think about how much better this one could be."

Jake could hear the excitement in her voice but he was not feeling the same. For all he knows, it just a couple of judges demeaning you. He gets belittled enough for being the younger brother.

"Mom, what if my story isn't good enough. Today I read my story in front of my class, and they laughed."

"Did it ever occur to you that they probably laughed because it was funny?"

Jake hadn't thought of that. He felt kind of silly for being embarrassed. He shouldn't have jumped to conclusions.

His mom was starting to convince Jake. Maybe she was right, maybe Jake should join the competition.

"Fine, I'll try. I'll talk to my English teacher tomorrow morning. Now, I'm going to watch some Netflix before dinner."

"After you do your homework right?"

Jake smiled and replied sarcastically.

"Right."

Chapter 5

Jake didn't tell Amanda about the competition yet. They didn't have English together so Jake didn't really have a chance. In the meantime, it was almost 7th period. Math, he would get to see his best friend again.

"You'll never believe what happened?"

"Hello, to you too." Amanda replied sarcastically.

"Hi. Guess."

"What?"

"I entered the writing competition!"

And for the first time in a while, Amanda was speechless. Jake never thought he'd see the day that Amanda couldn't find the right words to say. But that feeling didn't last long.

"I don't get it. Why is this big news."

Jake rolled his eyes. "This is not something I would usually do. Apparently I got an A+ on my story in writing class and Ms. Reaper recommended it to me."

"Really, how far did you get."

"Let's not get into details."

"So, you barely started."

"You're just jealous you don't have my genius."

"Yeah, that *must* be it."

"Okay class. Take your seats. Class is about to start." Ms. Smith said prompting the beginning of math class.

Jake wanted to be on his best behavior, but that was harder than he thought. It was a long time since he paid attention in class and an even longer time since he did the work. He could see Amanda noticed this when she asked:

"Are you sick?"

"No, I'm just trying to get on Ms. Smith's good side."

"Why?"

"I'm trying to raise my grade."

"Why?"

"Because-"

"Mr. Kale, why do we keep having this problem. Detention."

Ms. Smith had cut him off and Amanda didn't even get caught. Jake gave her the evil eye.

"Thanks a lot." He whispered obviously angry that she got away with it.

At least now he had an excuse to talk to Ms. Reaper.

It was last period and for the first time Jake was excited to stay an extra hour for school. He didn't dread the school bell sounding the end of the school day or the start of after school detention.

As he was walking to the wood door of room #217, he was thinking about Amanda. He realized she didn't even say sorry. Maybe she was jealous. But why would she be jealous of him, she was a straight A student in every single class and was one of the popular kids. What was she worried about.

He didn't have time to finish that thought before he put his hand to knock on the door and twisted the knob. Norman was already there at his desk doing homework.

"Again, Mr. Kale?" Ms. Reaper asked Jake. Jake smiled. As he gave her the slip he asked:

"After detention can I ask you a question?"

"Why not ask now before you sit down."

"Um, I would feel more comfortable tell you after."

"Okay, you may take a seat."

Even though Jake could hear the sternness in her voice, he could tell she was confused by the look in her eyes. Her befuddled look watched him all the way to his seat in the second row, the seat behind Norman.

Norman passed the first note.

> What was that all about

It continued back and forth.

> Don't worry about it, IT'S NONE OF YOUR BUSINESS

> Why are you being so secretive. Did you get on a fight?

> Can you a least TRY to stay out of it

> Can you a least try to tell me what that was about

Jake gave up at that point. He didn't right back.

At the end of detention, Norman walked out while giving him a bone chilling stare that sent goose bumps up his back. Jake didn't worry, Norman was practically harmless.

Once the nuisance was out of the classroom, Jake decided to make his move before Ms. Reaper left, and before anybody heard.

"Ms. Reaper?"

"Oh, yes, how can I forget about your question? You may proceed."

"I wanted to ask you for help on my story for the competition."

"Do you have a draft with you?"

"Yes, it's in my book bag." Jake was happy that he decided to write it last minute.

"Okay, let me read it."

Jake handed her the crumpled piece of paper, realizing the bad condition it was in. From habit, Jake just threw it into his book bag and hoped for the best. From the way Ms. Reaper held it, he probably shouldn't have done that. Even though she tried not to show it, Jake could see a glint of disgust in Ms. Reaper's eyes. Finally, Ms. Reaper began to read:

The Comic Book

I have a ~~secrete~~ secret. But you have to promise that you will never tell another single living soul about this. You must take it to your grave.

I live in a comic book. Yeah, I know that may be hard to believe but, every day, to get away from reality, I sneak away to my secret life in a comic.

After Ms. Reaper finished reading a paragraph's worth of content, she frowned obviously disappointed with the effort Jake put into it.

"Jake, you didn't even try. I know you could have done better. If you want help you should bring your best to the table. Try again."

Jake avoided Ms. Reaper's eye contact. Instead he looked to the floor, tracing the lines between the hardwood.

Ms. Reaper's eyes softened.

"The thing is Jake, your story has a good concept. You can elaborate from that. You have an active imagination, you can create an amazing story. I just know it."

"Thank you, Ms. Reaper."

"I'll tell you what, I'll give you until next week to wow me with a story and we'll sprout from there."

"Thank you, see you next week."

This didn't end up the way he expected but things seldom do.

Chapter 6

Next week Monday came by fast. Jake had been looking forward for the new week for a change. His mother noticed too when Jake asked if she could take him to school earlier.

"Why are you so eager to get to school today?"

"No specific reason. I'll eat breakfast in the car."

Jake felt his mother eyeing him at the front door. It made him feel uncomfortable as he reached for the knob.

As Jake went through the door, his mother stopped him.

"So, should I bring your book bag out for you?"

Jake could feel the hotness rush to his face as he went back inside to get his things.

Whenever Jake was in the car, he could always count on him and his mother having the same talk. It went by the same script every morning:

[Setting : Inside a black Lexus (Mother's car) ; Around 7:30 in the morning, 30 minutes before schools starts]

[Mother is doing her usual talk with her son, Jake, before school starts]

Mother turns down volume on radio still looking at road. She steals a look from her front mirror to get a peek of her son and quickly looks back at the cars in front of her. Jake falls into the trap and has nowhere to run

Mom: So, Jake, have you been doing well in school

Jake: Sure (rolls eyes)

Mom: Are you going to do better today

Jake: Sure (in bored sarcastic voice)

End Scene

But today the script was written a little differently:

[Setting: Inside a black Lexus (Mother's car); Around 7:00 in the morning, an hour before school starts]

[Mother is doing her usual talk with her son, Jake, before school starts but what happens when their conversation takes a detour]

Mother turns down volume on radio still looking at road. She steals a look from her front mirror to get a peek of her son and quickly looks back at the cars in front of her. Jake notices the confused looked on her face and knew what was coming.

Mom: So, Jake, why did you want to go to school earlier

Jake: I wanted my teacher to help me with my story (still with a breakfast bar in his mouth)

Mom: That sounds like a specific reason (referring to the comment Jake made earlier)

Jake: Yeah, I guess

Mom: You know I'm proud of you

Jake: (skeptical) Thanks

End Scene

Chapter 7

~~~~~~~~~~

After that very awkward talk in the car, Jake was relieved to finally be in school. As he said bye to his mother, he caught Amanda out of the corner of his eye. Amanda always came early because her father has to go to work. It was weird coming at the same time as her. To break the ice, Jake decided to talk to her before he went to Ms. Reaper.

Jake went over to the double doors that marked the entrance of the school. Before Amanda reached to pull the right door, Jake opened the left door for Amanda to go through. Instead of walking in and saying her thanks, Amanda eyed him suspiciously.

"What did you do this time?"

"What, I can't do something nice for my best friend without her thinking I did something wrong?"

She eyed Jake knowingly.

"Knowing you, No. Why are you here so early anyway?"

"For help on the writing competition."

"Everything is about the competition." Amanda rolled her eyes.

"You jealous?" Jake taunts

"You wish." Amanda snapped back.

They shared a small laugh. It was easy for them to be comfortable with each other.

"Are you going in?"

"Sure." she replied simply, but she didn't go through the side Jake held for her.

Amanda walked through the right side of the mahogany doors while Jake laughed silently and followed her.

Not a lot of people were there yet. It was mostly school staff and teachers roaming the hallways getting ready for the upcoming day.

"Where are you going?" Her words bringing Jake back to Planet Earth.

"Ms. Reaper."

She nodded and started to walk with him to the class.

Jake's mind kept drifting to math class. He didn't know why, it wasn't that significant. But for Jake it was everything. How was that fair? Jake forced it to stay at the back of his mind. He was probably overreacting.

Before he knew it, the pair was standing in front of the door that led to Ms. Reaper's room.

Amanda left, leaving Jake alone.

Jake walked into the warm room. Inside, it smelled like apple cinnamon. It was then that he noticed Ms. Reaper sitting at her desk. She looked smaller sitting at the big table.

"Hello." Jake almost whispered. Ms. Reaper looked up from her laptop and smiled at Jake.

"Good morning, Jake. Are you here for me to read your story?"

"Yes."

"Well, let's get started"

After Ms. Reaper read Jake's improved story, they got to work. Ms. Reaper was way more impressed this time. Although it needed a lot of work, it was obvious the amount of time and effort he put into it. In the short time they had together, Jake was able to continue what he thought was a dead end. Jake finally had respect for the authors he learned about in English. Guess they always made it sound easy. When time was running out, Jake began to pack his stuff and Ms. Reaper started talking about Jake's story.

"When a story ends, it only just begins" the teacher claimed.

Jake stared with blank eyes. In his mind, when a text says, "The End", it usually means the story is done and if you want a little spice you add "OR IS IT???".

"Listen Jake, your story is good, but if you want it to be great, rewrite it and add details and maybe even continue it. A run-of-the-mill story is 'fine the way it is', a great story takes you to a new world. And it is my job as a teacher to make sure my students don't settle for mediocrity."

"But-"

"Jake, listen to me. I know what the judges want. I know what it takes to be the best you can be. Now get to you first class, you don't want to be late."

Jake lingered in the classroom a little bit, but when he absolutely had no choice, he reached for the door.

"Thank you, Ms. Reaper."

Jake exited the room and left the door open.

Chapter 8

―⚬⚬⚬―

Jake decided to follow his teacher's advice. It took him a while, But Mrs. Reaper was right, his story was way better than he started with and Jake even felt proud.

It went a little like this:

The Comic Book

"I have a secret. Before you, I thought I was going to take it to my grave, but now I'm desperate in looking for someone I can trust. I never told another living soul and I'm not expecting you to blurt this out to anybody no matter how excited or scared you are.

"I live a double life. Every day after another depressing day of the normal world, I disappear to a secret world, in a comic book. It may be hard to believe now but I'm going to need you to trust me.

"Anyways, in the comic book world, I'm a well celebrated hero. Congratulated for saving the city from harm's way. But somehow, I've gotten myself into a dilemma. When I was in a fight with a giant robot, it somehow took my powers. Now, I'm gathering up a group of heroes to find out who's behind it and how to get my powers back. What do you say?"

Gravity stared at me. Her face showed that she had absolutely no idea what he was talking about. The silence didn't last long because after that all you can hear is Gravity laughing. The peculiar girl that thought she couldn't be more awkward was laughing. Maybe she was laughing at me because she was happy she wasn't the only loser around here. Or maybe because to her, I looked like a total oddball.

When she saw that my face didn't change from its serious expression, she stopped.

"Wait, are you actually serious? Andy, if you are playing with me, there's going to be a problem."

I slowly nodded. Gravity's face went blank. The paleness in her face said a lot but that didn't stop her from continuing.

"Even if you weren't lying, what would I be able to do. I don't know if you noticed, but I'm not super."

"That's what you think, but what you don't know is that you have a power that is stronger than anything in my world."

Gravity rolled her eyes like she heard it all before.

"And what's that, the power of being a freak?"

"No, the power of being different"

Gravity cringed at that. As cheesy as it was, it was one-hundred percent true.

"And if you were telling the truth where would I go and when?"

"I would tell you but I think you already know."

I could see the distant look in her eye. She knew.

I waited for her at the comic book store. Everyone else was already there. Jacob, who feels he'll be famous someday. Wendy, the tomboy who shows anybody up. And finally, Gravity, gamer and comic enthusiast.

"Are we ready to go?"

"What exactly do we do?" Wendy asked with her sass.

"You see this," I held up my favorite comic book to page 15, right in the middle. "One by one, we will jump into the book and we will be transported into another reality."

They didn't exactly look as impressed as I wanted them to but at least I got a few raised eyebrows.

"Ladies first." Jacob said with his voice cracking.

Gravity stepped forward while everyone stood back. Putting the book on the floor I said:

"Are you ready?"

She nodded hesitantly but jumped anyway. She disappeared in a flash of blue light. I smiled.

"Whose next?"

Chapter 9

"Hi Amanda."

It was loud in the cafeteria and Jake had to strain his voice to be heard over the crowd. Jake hasn't seen his best friend since the early encounter with her before his talk with Mrs. Reaper. This competition was taking most of his time.

"Hey." she responded as if she were waiting for something.

"What's wrong?" he said as he took a seat.

"Nothing." as she went back to eating her food.

Jake would have let that off the hook but he knew Amanda since kindergarten. Long enough to know that "Nothing" was something.

"Are you sure? Is it something I did?"

"Nothing." Except that time, it was harsher, but it was clear that she was waiting for something.

"Okay?" Jake answered wondering what that was all about.

Their conversation (if you could even call it that) didn't last long. Three girls that he hasn't seen before walked up to their table.

"Hey Andy." a blonde girl cheered with a high-pitched voice. Her long braid skipped with her as she jumped excitedly. Her pink off the shoulder shirt complimented a white skirt. Her image seemed harmless until, green eyes pierced through Jake as she realized that Jake was sitting at the table.

"Who's this?" her voice suddenly getting deeper. It gave Jake the chills.

"Hey guys. This is my *friend* Jake." Jake ignored the strain on the word and looked at the girl in front of him.

"K" her voice getting perky again. "Hi, my name is Bridget." now talking to Jake.

"Hello?" Jake said reluctantly, not really feeling welcome.

"This is Clio and Dominique." Bridget said gesturing to the two girls that began to take their seats.

Clio pulled a classic black hair ponytail away from her face that originally rested on her shoulder. She wore a black halter top with dark green jeans. Clio's eyes were a quiet hazel and by the way she avoided his eyes she was obviously the shy one. Dominique on the other hand had soft brown eyes and striking straight red hair that she wore out. She was wearing a bright yellow shirt tucked into khaki shorts with a brown leather belt. With her loud colors, it dawned on Jake that she was the confident one.

Jake didn't want to be rude, so he acknowledged them with a nod. The silence killed him, but Bridget couldn't be quiet for long.

"Andy-"

"It's Amanda," Amanda interrupted. Bridget rolled her eyes.

"Yeah, okay. Well, *Amanda*, what are you doing after school today. We are going to get ice-cream." she said gesturing to Clio and Dominique. "Do you want to come?"

Amanda stole a quick glance from Jake before answering. "Sure."

"Great! You can walk with us and my mother can drop you home."

Amanda smiled at the girls, but she wasn't happy. It was not a smile of complete content. She was trying to send a message to Jake, but he didn't know what.

"You can come too, if you want." Bridget said, now looking for Jake to answer.

Jake paused with shock, but it must have looked like hesitation because Bridget said:

"No really, it's okay."

"No, I'm fine."

He looked at Amanda to see if he chose the right answer but when he looked, her face was expressionless that didn't help him at all. Although, Bridget herself seemed happy with herself now.

Clio And Dominique sat quietly eating their lunch, seemingly afraid to say anything without permission. Heads down, they gave each other a quick glance, and went back to minding their own business. At that moment Jake knew something was up.

The rest of lunch went by quickly. Until the bell dismissed them for their next class. As Bridget and her friends got up she said, "By the way Andy, Happy Birthday." The other two girls nodded as the group walked away.

Amanda snuck another glance at Jake, this time angry, "Thanks," she said to the girls while staring a hole into the boy.

"At least someone remembered." as she began to leave the table.

Chapter 10

─────∽∽∽∽∽∽∽─────

How careless could I be? Amanda was my best friend and I just forgot about her. I could really be dense sometimes.

That's what Jake was thinking about instead of listening to Ms. Pradesh drone on about the difference between mitosis and meioses. The clues were all there. She was angry about something in the beginning because he didn't say anything about her birthday and Bridget, Clio, and Dominique invited her to ice cream to celebrate her special day.

Really how careless can I be?

"Jake pay attention." Ms. Pradesh called.

New kids would probably take advantage of Ms. Pradesh. She was a short woman and frail at that. She was not much older than most teachers at school but see definitely wasn't one of the youngest. But people who have been here longer know that once you're on Ms. Pradesh's bad side, there is no coming back. So when Ms. Pradesh gave Jake a warning look, he listened immediately.

Honestly, for Jake, it was a good distraction from whatever feud he has with Amanda after lunch. Jake knew that he was in big trouble even though nothing has happened yet. Especially since he had math next period.

Chapter 11

———∽∿∽———

"You're late Mr. Kale, again. But I can't say I'm surprised."
"Sorry, Mrs. Smith, it won't happen again."
"You bet it won't happen again or you'll be in detention. See you this afternoon."

Jake was going to take his usual seat next to Amanda but he came to find the seat taken by a girl he didn't recognize. The only seat left was the one in the front along with the "eager" students. The last thing Jake needed was to be called on.

Jake slowly walked to the seat. He looked up at Amanda. She was looking at him ,but as soon as their eyes met, she turned away.

"Hurry up Jake, we don't have all day"

Jake quickly sat down and waited for the lesson to begin. Jake just couldn't wait for the class to be over. He couldn't wait until detention came around.

When the bell rang, Amanda was out before Jake had a chance to talk to her. As Amanda stormed off, Jake put his stuff together to get ready for detention. This day was really starting to get on Jake's nerves.

Chapter 12

"Why are we back here again?" Ms. Reaper says disappointed.

All Jake could do was shrug and walk to his seat with his head down. He had a lot to think about. When Jake looked up, he saw Ms. Reaper looking at him with a confused look. She slowly looked away not even trying to hide the befuddled expression.

Jake looked around. Like usual Norman was there, but what surprised Jake was who sat in the four seats behind him. It was Amanda, Bridget, Clio, and Dominique. Amanda didn't meet his eyes but Bridget sure did. Her green eyes looked anything but inviting. Jake changed his position to look at Norman and waved. Norman gladly waved back.

One thing Jake did not want to do was work. His mind was racing with why Amanda had detention and if she was still mad at him. Apparently she wasn't because a few minutes later she came up to him and asked to sit next to him

Taken by surprise he let her, but not before he said Happy Birthday. Amanda laughed and took her seat.

"It's okay. It's not that serious anyway."

"Of course it is. Your turning-"

"No talking please. You should know better Jake." Ms. Reaper scolded, eyeing Jake.

"Sorry." Jake replied respectfully.

He looked back at Amanda and gave her a thumbs up and mouthed *"Are we good?"*

Amanda knew just what it meant and nodded. They looked at each other and both looked to the group of three at the same time.

Brittany looked menacing. They slowly looked back to the front. They were silent for a few seconds before they started laughing. It felt so good to laugh. But that quickly ended when Ms. Reaper gave them a look.

Jake tore a piece of paper out of his notebook and began writing.

What did you get in here for.

Amanda took a look at the piece of paper and took a deep breath. She flipped the paper around.

Brittany had a genius idea of skipping class by asking to go to the bathroom at the same time. We were caught.

The conversation continued.

Are you guys still friends?

Amanda needed some time to answer that one.

I'm not sure about that.

Why did you do it? It doesn't sound like something you would do?

Because some of my other friends were busy.

That made Jake feel guilty. He hasn't been talking to Amanda as much because the competition. The competition! Jake has nearly forgotten all about his story. But surely his best friend was more important.

I'm sorry.

Before Amanda could write anything back. Ms. Reaper called him to the front of the classroom. Amanda and Jake exchanged glances for the second time that day.

As he walked up there, he could feel the piercing stares of all six people in the room including Ms. Reaper.

"Are you working on those revisions I asked you to work on?" She asked loud enough for only him to hear.

"I was planning on working on them at home. After school."

"Right. You may sit down now."

Jake didn't know what to take from her facial expression. Her face monotone as well as her voice. He never seen her like this. It scared him.

Jake slowly turned around and walked back to his seat. Amanda looked at him with a look of confusion and all he could do back was shrug.

Chapter 13

—⚬⚬⚬—

Jake was glad that Amanda was talking to him again. But the long run was not over yet. He still had a bunch of revisions to make and an angry teacher to worry about. Even though he rather be done with everything he had no choice but to keep going.

When he got home instead of seeing his mother at the kitchen table, he saw his brother watching television. Drake looked up at him and revealed that their mother was still at work and wouldn't be back until late.

"But why are you here so early? Don't you usually have Debate or Basketball or... something?"

"Well first of all its Wednesday so I would have had a student council meeting. Second, it was canceled for reasons you wouldn't understand."

Jake rolled his eyes at that. Drake always assumed that Jake "wouldn't understand". It got on his nerves that Drake thought he was so much better than him. But he never fought back. He knew it would never end well for him. So all he did was nod.

"Mom left us money for pizza but for now you can take a bag of chips from the pantry."

"Don't tell me what to do." Jake said defiantly as he walked toward the pantry.

Now it was Drake's turn to roll his eyes.

After that, Drake went back to watching his show and Jake took a bag of barbecue and went to work on his story.

Jake sat there for a few minutes to let the creative juices flow. Once he knew what he needed, he was there revising for who knows how long. The only thing that distracted Jake from his thoughts was when he heard the doorbell and Drake yell "Pizza's here!"

"Coming!" Jake yelled back. On his way to the kitchen Jake reached for his story. Drake could probably tell him how to spice it up. Although he could be annoying, he was a genius.

Coming into the kitchen, the smell of cheesy tomato sauce goodness made Jake's mouth water.

"So what you up to little brother?"

Jake didn't even say a word. He passed his brother the paper and went straight for a slice. He didn't even realize how hungry he was until he took a bite.

Drake looked at him with a sarcastic look on his face.

"You okay there?"

Jake just pointed to the paper and said "Read".

And that's what Drake did.

Jake looked at the expressions on his face. Turning from skeptical to engaged, to pleased, to confused.

"Do you like it?"

"Where's the rest of it?"

"I ended it on a cliff hanger to make it more interesting. But do you like it?"

"It's amazing. What is it for?"

"I'm joining this writing competition. My teacher recommended it to me."

"Well with that story, I think you could win."

"Thanks."

Drake reached for his first slice as Jake reached for his third. It felt good to hear that his brother was proud of him. Drake was always doing noteworthy things and Jake was usually getting attention for all the wrong reasons. But maybe after this story, that wouldn't be the case.

After his third slice, Jake poured himself a cup of juice. He was thinking of watching YouTube videos until he fell asleep. Leaning against the counter, Jake let his mind run wild. But the sound of a key unlocking a door alerted him to realize that his mother was home.

"How are my boys doing?"

"Good." Jake said expecting Drake to say the same but to Jake's surprise, Drake was completely silent.

"I need to talk to you," his mother said pointed directly towards Drake.

This confused Jake. His mother only did that when Jake was in trouble and to him the thought of Drake ever getting in trouble was nonexistent.

"Jake please go to your room." Although his mother was being polite, Jake knew it wasn't a request, it was an order.

Without a fight, Jake headed to his room. Instead of closing the door all the way, he left it open just a sliver, barely noticeable so he wouldn't get in trouble.

At first all he heard was silence. His mother must be doing one of her famous death stares that can freeze anybody from miles away.

"Tell me why I got a call from your principal telling me that you were suspended from student council."

Again silence haunted the kitchen. Jake didn't need to sneak a look to know that Drake was avoiding eye contact. He knows that's what he would be doing in his shoes. This was the situation Jake "wouldn't understand". Honestly it hurt him that Drake didn't trust him with that information. He discarded this and kept listening.

"Can you explain to me *why*?"

More silence. It was suffocating.

"Before you have grand kids, please hurry up."

Jake couldn't help but feel bad. He's been there so many times before but hearing his brother go through it hurt way more.

"Okay, you can tell me when you're ready but in the meantime, let me hold onto your phone for you. It must be a distraction from remembering what happened."

It was a few more minutes of silence until I heard footsteps go towards the room next to mine. Drake's room. The door silently closed.

Chapter 14

Jake could still feel the tension the next day. Drake seemed to never make eye contact with anyone. Especially not his mother.

When they got the chance to be alone, Jake nudged Drake with this foot to get his attention. Drake looked up with sadness in his eyes.

"I 'wouldn't understand'."

Drake rolled his eyes which would have infuriated Jake, but he understood where he was coming from.

"Why didn't you tell me you were suspended?"

Drake looked surprised, then angry.

"Nobody told you to eavesdrop."

"Nobody told me not to."

Drake rolled his eyes for the second time. Jake chose to ignore it again and kept pressing.

"Why didn't you tell me?"

"Why would I need to?"

Drake was starting to get on Jake's nerves. He used all of his discipline, not to jump over the table and use Drake's morning bacon to slap Drake in the face. Instead, Jake took a deep breath.

"Because I'm your brother. You lied to me and you don't even care. I'm starting to regret ever feeling bad for you."

That caught Drake's attention. for the first time that morning, Drake looked straight into Jake's eyes. But in his eyes was not repentance, but anger.

"I don't need you to feel sorry for me. What I need is for you to leave me alone."

With that Drake got up furiously, and walked away.

"Aren't you going to put your plate in the sink." Jake called after him snarkily.

All Jake got as a response was a slam of Drake's bedroom door.

"So that's a "no" then." Jake said, adding wood to the fire.

"Shut up."

All Jake could do was laugh. He knew it was wrong to annoy his brother in the state he was in, but he couldn't help it. Not too long after, Jake's mother reminded Jake it was time for him to be dropped off.

Chapter 15

The car was silent. That was not normal for the Kale family, especially not for their mother. To Jake this was a terrifying experience. This has never happened before. He would do anything for the script that they usually followed. At least that was something recognizable.

Drake stared out the window blankly. He was expressionless.

Jake had to do something. If not, he was sure he was going to suffocate on the tension.

"What's better? Pancakes or Waffles?"

"What?" Drake replied sounding honestly confused.

His mother brought up one eyebrow while keeping her eyes on the road.

"Which one is better?"

Drake looked skeptical.

"Why?"

"I just want to know. Personally, I think waffles are better."

"Don't they taste the same." Now their mother was joining in.

"Yeah, so."

"So how can one be better than the other."

"Just because it is." Jake shrugged.

"Pancakes are better. That's why there are pancake art challenges rather than waffle art challenges." Drake answered.

"No, I think waffles are better because you can put more syrup in them. I have a huge sweet tooth." Mom smiled.

Jake successfully turned the situation around. It was kind of fun actually. Talking about something as childish as this was giving the day a bright filter.

Throughout the rest of the car ride all you could hear was laughter and the occasional question.

"If you pinch yourself and it hurts, does that mean you are too strong or too weak?" or "Why is a boxing ring square if a ring is supposed to be circular?"

Jack almost didn't even notice when his mother pulled up to his school. He thought about how the rest of the car ride would be like without him. But he couldn't think about that now. He had a whole day in ahead of him.

Chapter 16

"I'm impressed." Ms. Reaper said after reading the story.

It was only five minutes before the bell rings, but Jake just had to show Ms. Reaper the hard work he had done.

"I'll submit this in as soon as possible." Ms. Reaper smiled.

The day was off to a great start. He relieved the tension in the car and Jake's story was finally done after a lot of hard work. He didn't want to jinx it but Jake just felt it was going to be a good day.

Time was ticking. There were three minutes for him to get to his first period class. He rushed out the door after thanking his teacher properly. His next class was on the third floor and he was on the first. He raced to Art with a few seconds to spare.

He sat in his usual seat in the back. From there, he could see anything and everything in the classroom. He has never noticed before but in the third row, two over, was Bridget. She was talking to somebody next to her. There was no way Jake could find out what they were saying from two rows back. But apparently, he wouldn't have had the chance anyway because at that moment Ms. Kelly walked in.

Ms. Kelly wasn't an angry woman if you didn't not give her a reason to raise her voice. She was quite nice and funny but not slow to give out detentions to those who rub her the wrong way.

As soon as the woman took a step into the classroom, the light hum of the room fell immediately.

"Glad I got your attention." Ms. Kelly noted, lightening the mood of the group.

"Good Morning class!"

"Good Morning!" the class said back some sounding tired and some sounding like they had way too much coffee. Regardless Ms. Kelly beamed at her students for the morning.

"Today we are working on one point perspective."

The class moaned.

"Relax. Settle down. Hey." she waited until the class's attention was on her again, "I feel like once I explain you might not think of it as a silly art project."

Although the class's attention was still on Ms. Kelly, Jake's mind wandered elsewhere. All Jake could think about was what was Bridget and the mystery girl.

The class broke into cheers which broke Jake out of his trance.

He tapped the person next to him, he believed his name was Raquel.

"What happened?"

"The principal is choosing one project that is the best. The winning project will be in the school newspaper."

"So."

Raquel rolled his eyes at that.

"So the class with the winning student gets to have a party of their choosing."

Now that was a game changer.

Jake looked back at Bridget. She looked like she was planning something. The smirk on her face said it all.

Jake had to find out what she was planning and if it were related to the message she was telling the mystery girl. And more importantly if it was related to Amanda.

Chapter 17

―⁓⁓⋄⋄⋄⁓⁓―

"Do not get involved."

Lunch time came fast and Jake couldn't wait to tell Amanda what he found out. But Amanda wasn't as pleased as Jake thought she would be.

"Why not?"

"Because you're only going to make it worse. Besides, I don't want anything to do with her. You don't even know what they were actually talking about. It could be insignificant."

"But what if it isn't?"

"But what if it is?"

Jake sighed heavily. He knew Amanda was more good-natured than himself. She wouldn't go for it even if she knew for sure. But he also knew it would hurt her if he went behind her back. So maybe it would be a good idea to put this on the back burner

"So, did you hear about the art competition."

"Yeah."

"I think you could win."

Art was Amanda's hidden talent. Ever since she was little Amanda was able to draw anything with ease. It was something she rarely told anybody. Jake still didn't know why she would keep something like this unknown but he respected her word and didn't bring it up much.

"You think?"

"I know."

"You know, I haven't read the story you're handing in."

"You never asked."

"I'm asking now."

Jake playfully rolled his eyes. He reached into his backpack to look for the rough draft but before he could take it out a person stepped up to the table. Jake recognized her as the girl Bridget was talking to in the morning. Jake immediately went into high alert.

"Hi, can I sit here?"

Jake and Amanda exchanged glances. Jake shook his head slightly, not noticeable enough for mystery girl to notice.

"Sure." Amanda said ignoring the warnings Jake gave earlier. "What's your name?"

"Emily. I'm new here." she said shyly but Jake wasn't buying the innocent girl act for a second. But to amuse her he decided to play her game.

"Which school did you come from."

"Lincoln Middle. It's in Jersey."

"Interesting." Amanda replied eyeing Jake as if he had done something wrong. "Why did you come here?"

"My mom got a promotion in her law firm and we all had to move over here."

"We?"

"My mom, my dad and my older brother."

"Do you miss it over there?"

"Yeah all the time. All my friends are over there."

"Aww."

Emily smiled at this.

"It's okay. I'm fine. I just want you guys to act natural. What were you guys talking about before this?"

"Oh, just about the art competition and Jake's story."

Now it was Jake's turn to eye Amanda. That was way too much information to give at once but Amanda continued to ignore him.

"Oh, I heard about that. I'm so excited."

"Really? Are you good at art?"

Emily blushed.

"I wouldn't say I was the best but I'm not bad."

Now this was really getting interesting.

"Do you have any pictures you can show us? I'd love to see what you can do."

Emily looked embarrassed but excited at the same time.

"Do you really?"

"Yeah." Amanda smiled.

Emily opened her binder and flipped to a drawing of what seemed to be her and her family in colored pencil.

Jake didn't want to admit it but it was beautiful and he could tell that Amanda felt the same way.

When Jake looked up at her he could tell from just her eyes. She felt intimidated.

Chapter 18

Amanda denied it. Of course she would never admit to being unsettled. She said that if she was meant to win she would win. But to Jake she didn't sound too convincing. Just because she said it, doesn't mean she believes it.

"Besides, Emily is our friend. I don't want to hurt her."

Jake rolled his eyes at that. How could Amanda think Emily is her friend? Amanda had morals Jake just didn't understand.

"Plus you already promised you wouldn't get involved. And you *never* break a promise."

That made Jake feel guilty. He may not have had strong morals but it was true. He never breaks a promise. And he didn't want this situation to be the first time he does. Maybe he will actually watch this play out, but the second Amanda says the word, Hades reigns will break loose.

"Fine, I won't get involved."

"Thank you."

Just then the bell rang announcing the end of lunch.

Chapter 19

"I'm home."

"Good for you."

Drake was on the couch seemingly taking a nap. Or trying. All Jake can do is roll his eyes and laugh.

"Mom's not home yet?"

"Do you see her here?"

"Ohhh feisty."

Now it is Drake's turn to roll his eyes.

"She's going to be home soon. Just relax."

Drake didn't have to tell Jake twice. It's the first time in a long time that Jake doesn't have homework. He didn't have anything to do, so relax he shall.

Jake let himself to the snacks and disappeared into his room. And he did so for hours before realizing how late it was. He decided to investigate. He walked into the living room to find Drake passed out on the couch. He obviously didn't realize the time either so Jake decided to wake him up.

"What do you want from me?"

"Didn't you say Mom was going to be home soon?"

"Yeah, it's only been five minutes. Relax."

"More like three hours."

"Wait what? You got to be kidding me." Drake said after looking at the time on the clock.

"I over slept."

"That's all you can think about right now?" Jake rolled his eyes. "Where is Mom?"

"Relax I'm sure she's fine."

Jake walked towards the house phone.

"Yeah, I'm sure she's fine with three miss calls."

"What?!" Drake quickly got up from the couch and stood next to Jake to see what he was talking about.

"How come you didn't come and pick it up?"

"Hey don't pin this all on me. You did this to yourself."

"Argh!"

"Wow that's an interesting sound. You've got to teach that to me sometime."

Drake turned and rolled his eyes. He picked up the landline and quickly punched in their mother's number.

"Mom?... What happened?... No, we're okay. How about you? ... Sorry. ... Okay."

Drake hung up after talking to his mom.

"What happened, what did she say?"

"Well she got off work late and now she's in traffic. Nothing drastic. But she is definitely not happy that I didn't pick up right away. She's questioning how responsible I am."

"Oh, she is big mad?"

"Stop it, its not funny. Not everything has to be a joke."

"But you make it so easy."

Drake rolled his eyes again.

"Mom doesn't know what time she is coming home. She told us we can eat takeout."

"At least one good thing came out of this."

Drake rolled his eyes again.

"Whatever. Chinese?"

"Yeah."

When their mother came home she did not look pleased. She was using her death stare again to bore holes into Drake who was eating at the counter.

"Jake. Room."

"Wow, I don't even get a 'hello' anymore?"

"Jake." Their mother spoke with her warning voice, her eyes never leaving Drake.

Before leaving he took a look at Drake. He looked terrified. He couldn't blame him. Their mom looked terrifying.

He walked to his room reluctantly. This time he didn't risk leaving his door open. He didn't want to get in trouble, but even more he didn't want to get on Drake's nerves. He knew he was already stressed. He will stick to their "playful banter". At least that's what their mom calls it.

Even though the door was closed. Jake can tell Drake was getting a beat down in a battle he never got to fight. Jake wanted to do something but he knew that wasn't the best idea.

Maybe one day he would get that courage.

Chapter 20

"The results are in."

Jake and his family were at the event along with Amanda who wanted to be there and Ms. Reaper who made an appearance as the MC. Jake was nervous beyond belief. Amanda must have noticed because she gave him a reassuring nod that brought his confidence levels up.

Jake played with the cuff of his tux to take his mind off his nervousness. It didn't work.

"A drum roll please."

As the tension rose, Jake tried to ignore the anxiousness by replacing it with happy thoughts.

"And the…"

Either way I going to get ice cream so there is nothing to worry about.

"Winner is…"

For once I am at an academic event where I am not getting in trouble.

"Jake Kale."

And I- Wait what!

Everyone started to look at the boy who was deemed the winner. Amanda nudged him to get him out of his trance.

Jake slowly got up and made his way to the podium to collect what would be his first ever trophy.

"Not only will Jake be getting this trophy, but his short story will be on the front cover of the local newspaper."

Jake stood next to the judges' table and smiled for the press.

"Congratulations Mr. Kale." Jake headed back to his seat. His jitters had disappeared. His family was welcoming him with large smiles. Amanda gave him two thumbs up and after the madness of the event, Ms. Reaper came to congratulate him personally.

"I saw that you were a little surprised when I mentioned you as the winner."

"Yeah, I wasn't really expecting that. It caught me off guard."

Ms. Reaper laughed.

"I could see that. How do you feel? Happy? Excited?"

"I honestly don't know how to feel about it. But I know I shouldn't worry about it. If the judges actually believed it was a good story than other people should like it too. And if they don't, it's their loss."

"That's a good way to look at it. Well have a good weekend."

"Thank you, you too."

Jake couldn't wait to celebrate with his family and Amanda. He always got an Oreo sundae and his brother always got a chocolate cone with chocolate sprinkles. speaking of his brother. He hasn't seen Drake since Jake stood up to go to the podium. He decided to ask Amanda.

"Hey Amanda, where did Drake go?"

"Last time I saw him, he said he needed to go to the bathroom, but that was a long time ago. He should be back by now."

"Thank you." Jake started towards the bathrooms.

"Oh and Jake..."

Jake stopped in his tracks.

"He told me to tell you he was proud of you."

Jake ran to the bathroom door and opened it. It was seemingly empty but Jake wasn't that gullible.

"Drake? Are you in here?"

He checked the stalls for feet and in the last one was a familiar pair of Vans.

"Drake? Why are you in here?"

"Leave me alone."

"We're about to leave for ice cream and we're not going to leave without you."

"Maybe not you but I know some people who would like too."

"What are you talking about?"

"Never mind."

Drake forcefully opened the stall door and left the bathroom which left Jake there alone. That whole time Drake did not look at him what so ever. There was something Drake was upset about but Jake couldn't seem to put his finger on it. But he will find out if it was the last thing he did.

Chapter 21

"Hey, can I come in?"

"Go away."

"I'll take that as a yes."

Jake bust through his brother's door. Jake and his family had just gotten home from their celebration but Drake seemed out of it and went straight to his bedroom.

"Get out of my room."

"I will... right after you tell me what's wrong with you."

Drake groaned. He was obviously not in the mood for talking.

"Can you just leave me alone? Why can't you go away."

"Why can't you just tell me what's wrong?"

"If I tell you will you go away?"

"I won't be here any longer than I have to. It smells like older brother in here."

Drake rolled his eyes but readjusted himself on the bed so that he was facing Jake. Drake's face suddenly turned serious which scared Jake. That was very different from his happy go lucky attitude. Drake took a deep breath and so did Jake. Jake could already tell that it was going to be a heavy conversation.

"I'm jealous."

"I'm sorry, what?"

"Jake." Drake said using his warning tone that he probably inherited from their mother.

"I'm sorry continue."

"Right now you are doing so well. You are out there accomplishing things and you are improving. It seems like you are doing everything right. And I am just the opposite. I am getting into more and more trouble with mom and even more trouble in school and it seems no matter how hard I try to fix that, it gets worse. What I said in the bathroom, that's what I meant. I meant that some people are just so tired of me right now, that including mom. That's why I'm so upset."

"You done."

"Are you serious?"

"No, the question is 'are *you* serious'. How do you think I feel most of the time. You are the amazing older brother with impossible expectations to live up to.. I am constantly being compared to you from every degree. But, it is hard competing with someone who is captain of almost every school club and who is always at the top of the class. I am always in your shadow. I can't believe you would be that insensitive. That's why *I'm* so upset."

Drake suddenly looked shy.

"I had no idea. You are always so positive about everything. Why didn't you tell me?"

"Because I wasn't stupid enough to be angry or sad about something so insignificant. Either way you are my brother and I know that you wouldn't want me to feel that way. When I'm in a tough situation like that, I usually think 'What would Drake do' because I know you would look on the bright side and do the right thing. But, right now, you are really letting me down."

"I'm sorry. I didn't know you felt that way. I didn't know I was such a horrible brother."

"Get a hold of yourself, that's not what I was trying to say. You are not a horrible brother. You are just acting a horrible way. It will pass and you will learn from your mistakes. I just want that brother I can look up to again, that's why I came here in the first place."

"Is that true?"

Jake nodded.

"Thank you, I really needed to hear that, especially from you. I'm glad you wouldn't let me slip though."

"That's what brothers are for."

Jake smiled and headed for the door. But before he left he couldn't help himself.

"And thank you."

"For what"?

"For being proud of me."

Jake left without another word.

Chapter 22

"I won."

"No doubt about it."

It has been a few days since Jake's story has been on the newspaper. His fifteen seconds of fame has been good while it lasted but now it was Amanda's time to shine.

"Emily is an amazing artist and I thought that maybe she would win."

"You shouldn't have let her psyche you out. And speaking of the new girl."

Emily walked up to the table looking genuinely cheerful about something.

"Amanda congratulations, and you too Jake of course."

Jake looked confused. He barely knew Emily but the competition was over. Why was she being so nice?

"Thank you, I'm so surprised that I even won."

"Don't be. You are such a talented artist. Way better than I'll ever be."

"Don't say that." Amanda blushed.

Jake sat silently while the two girls gushed over each other. It wasn't because he was angry, it was because he was confused. If Emily was sincere that would mean that Bridget wasn't planning anything to begin with. Which would mean he was all twisted up about nothing. Which would mean Amanda was right, there was nothing to be worried about.

"Right Jake."

Jake was startled. Emily had just brought Jake into reality and Amanda and Emily were both looking expectant for an answer.

"Um... I wasn't listening."

Amanda turned to Emily.

"He does that a lot. It's like he is on a different planet."

Emily laughed and turned towards Jake.

"I'm the same way too. I usually think about the craziest things when I supposed to be focused on something else. But it helps with my creativity."

"Yeah, a lot of times my story ideas come from my daydreams."

"That's exactly what I do except I make them into drawings. Looking at my pictures is like a segway into the madness of my brain."

"That's so cool."

The three continued to talk as a group. Jake learned that Emily wasn't so bad after all. She even liked some of the same things Jake liked. Jake was actually disappointed when the bell rang announcing the end of lunch.

When Emily left, Amanda stood up and gave Jake the 'I told you so' look.

"Don't you dare say it?

"I don't know what you're talking about." as she walked away.

It was going to be a long day.

One-day people will admire that I daydream so much. They would all gather around to hear them.

His thoughts were more accurate than he imagined...